For Daisy:
Sports Superstar – MH

For Sports Superstar
Jane 10536 – EO

SIMON & SCHUSTER

First published in Great Britain in 2020 by Simon & Schuster UK Ltd • 1st Floor, 222 Gray's Inn Road, London, WC1X 8HB • A CBS Company • Text copyright © 2020 Morag Hood • Illustrations copyright © 2020 Ella Okstad • The right of Morag Hood and Ella Okstad to be identified as the author and illustrator of this work has been asserted by them in accordance with the Copyright, Designs and Patents Act, 1988 • All rights reserved, including the right of reproduction in whole or in part in any form • A CIP catalogue record for this book is available from the British Library upon request.

978-1-4711-8813-8 (HB) • 978-1-4711-8814-5 (PB) • 978-1-4711-8815-2 (eBook)

Printed in China • 10 9 8 7 6 5 4 3 2 1

Sophie Johnson: sports superstar

Morag Hood and Ella Okstad

SIMON & SCHUSTER
London   New York   Sydney   Toronto   New Delhi

My name is
Sophie Johnson
and I am great at sports.
In fact, I am a
sports superstar.

Like many of the best sports superstars,
I am getting ready for a Big Race.

This race is probably the longest,
hardest race anyone has ever tried to do **ever**.

Mum says that she can help me with my training, but I don't think I need her.

I **am** the sports superstar around here after all.

I know everything
there is to know about
bending and stretching,

and I can move
my arms and legs
very fast.

I don't have time to listen to Mum.

I am much too busy working on my Excellent Plan for the race.

There are lots of important things to think about if you want to become a champion.

Sports superstars like me need to eat very special food.

And after all that training and eating, plenty of rest is important too.

You can't become a sports superstar like me
if you tire yourself out bothering about silly things,
like mess and crumbs.

Because when it comes to race day,

a sports superstar must be ready for anything.

I mustn't be distracted by the roar of the crowd, however excited they are to see me.

I have a race to run and every second counts.

It's lucky I am so good at concentrating actually.

I mustn't let anyone catch up with me…

...otherwise who knows what could happen!

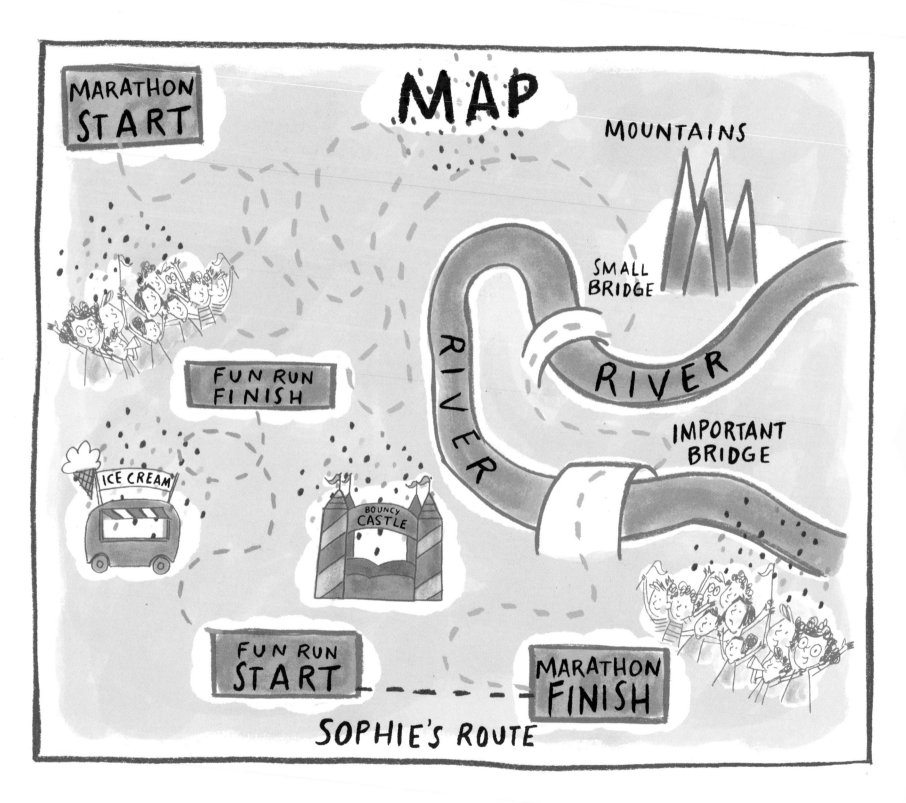

There is no stopping a true sports superstar.

Really, it's a good job I'm here.
Some people don't know the first thing
about how to run a race properly.

GO SOPHIE!

VICTORY
DANCE!

GO FAST

That's why they need me –
Sophie Johnson, Sports Superstar.

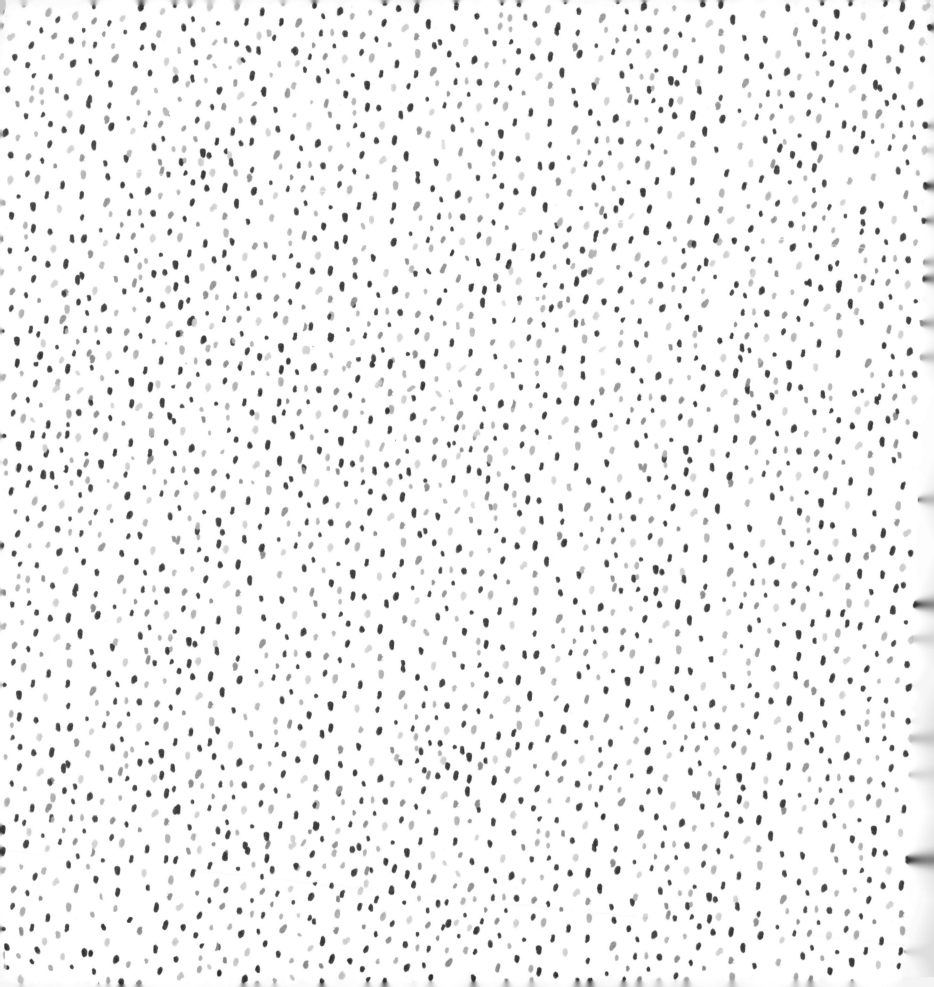

Sophie Johnson:
SPÖRTS
SuperStar

RO

221

4

This

The
a fu.